DRIVE THRU

THE CHASE FOR CHEESE

by Harriet Brundle

BEARPORT
PUBLISHING

Minneapolis, Minnesota

Credits

All images are courtesy of Shutterstock.com, unless otherwise specified. With thanks to Getty Images, Thinkstock Photo, and iStockphoto.

Front Cover - John Gold, Shurik76, digitmilk, MSPhotographic, 2&3 - Oxy_gen, 4&5 - paprika, 6&7 - Dagmar hijmans, Sara Winter, Irina Petrusevich, Michelle Lee Photography, Natali Zakharova, svariophoto, 8&9 - Toa55, Macrovecto, 10&11 - ChiccoDodiFC, Svitlana Slobodianiuk, 12&13 - Oleksandr Yakoniuk, Diachuk Vasyl, WinWin artlab, 14&15 - Melting Spot, Niloo, Paolo Sartorio, 16&17 - Liv friis-larsen, JPC-PROD, Natali Zakharova, HappyPictures, 18&19 - ViDCan, Ba_peuceta, 20&21 - MagicBones, Ian Luck, Ann in the uk, 22&23 - Alluvion Stock, Melissa Patton, SIMEC STUDIO, Jabrinki Art

Library of Congress Cataloging-in-Publication Data

Names: Brundle, Harriet, author.
Title: The chase for cheese / by Harriet Brundle.
Description: Fusion books. | Minneapolis, Minnesota : Bearport Publishing Company, [2022] | Series: Drive thru | Includes bibliographical references and index.
Identifiers: LCCN 2021011422 (print) | LCCN 2021011423 (ebook) | ISBN 9781647479442 (library binding) | ISBN 9781647479527 (library binding) | ISBN 9781647479602 (ebook)
Subjects: LCSH: Cheese--Juvenile literature. | Cheesemaking--Juvenile literature.
Classification: LCC SF271 .B74 2022 (print) | LCC SF271 (ebook) | DDC 637/.3--dc23
LC record available at https://lccn.loc.gov/2021011422
LC ebook record available at https://lccn.loc.gov/2021011423

© 2022 Booklife Publishing
This edition is published by arrangement with Booklife Publishing.

North American adaptations © 2022 Bearport Publishing Company. All rights reserved. No part of this publication may be reproduced in whole or in part, stored in any retrieval system, or transmitted in any form or by any means, electronic, mechanical, photocopying, recording, or otherwise, without written permission from the publisher.

For more information, write to Bearport Publishing, 5357 Penn Avenue South, Minneapolis, MN 55419. Printed in the United States of America.

CONTENTS

Hop in the Cheese Wheels 4
The Chase for Cheese 6
Making Cheese 8
From Milk to Curds 10
Time to Age 12
How Does It Taste? 14
Blue Cheese 16
Soft Cheese 18
Hard Cheese 20
Cheese Time! 22
Glossary 24
Index 24

HOP IN THE CHEESE WHEELS

Hi, I'm Coty! Welcome to my food truck, the Cheese Wheels, where I make tasty cheesy meals. Which one would you like to try?

* MENU *

Cheese pizza

Macaroni and cheese

Grilled cheese

Chocolate cheesecake

THE CHASE FOR CHEESE

Cheese is made in many places, including the Netherlands, Germany, France, and Switzerland.

Cheese can be made using milk from cows, sheep, and goats.

There are different kinds of cheese. Cheeses can be soft or hard. Some cheeses are super smelly, and some are even blue!

CHEDDAR

GORGONZOLA

MOZZARELLA

MAKING CHEESE

Because most cheese is made from animal milk, the first step is to get the milk from the animals. Then, the milk is heated to kill bad **bacteria**.

Some farmers use machines to milk cows.

FROM MILK TO CURDS

Next, something called **rennet** is added to the milk. The rennet makes the milk **curdle**.

CURDLED MILK

When the milk curdles, it forms some **solid** chunks called curds. It also has a **liquid** called whey. The whey is taken away, leaving just the curds.

TIME TO AGE

The curds are salted to add flavor and to help the cheese stay fresh. Then, the curds are shaped into blocks or wheels. These shapes become cheese.

Cheese being shaped

Many cheeses must sit to **age**. They might sit for weeks or even years. They are kept in places that are not too hot and not too cold.

Some cheeses age in caves.

HOW DOES IT TASTE?

Parmesan aging

The taste of cheese depends on where it ages and how long it sits. Cheeses that age longer usually have a stronger flavor.

After the cheese ages, it is ready to be packed up and sold!

BLUE CHEESE

Some cheeses are made a little differently. Blue cheese has a different kind of bacteria added to it.

GORGONZOLA BLUE CHEESE

ROQUEFORT BLUE CHEESE

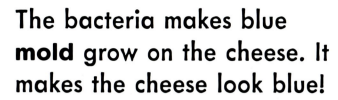

The bacteria makes blue **mold** grow on the cheese. It makes the cheese look blue!

Some blue cheeses are smelly!

SOFT CHEESE

Soft cheeses are not aged for as long as hard cheeses. Some soft cheeses do not need to age at all!

Fresh mozzarella is not usually aged.

Brie cheese ages for about four weeks. A hard edge forms on the outside, but the cheese stays soft on the inside.

Soft cheeses include mozzarella, feta, and Brie.

HARD CHEESE

There are many kinds of hard cheese, including cheddar, Swiss, and Parmesan.

You might have tried Parmesan sprinkled on pasta or pizza.

Hard cheeses can age for months or years. Some kinds of Parmesan sit for two or three years—or even longer!

PARMESAN ON PIZZA

GLOSSARY

age to change over time and become better

bacteria tiny living things, too small to see, that can grow on foods

curdle to separate into lumps and liquid

liquid a thing that flows and has no set shape, such as water

mold a growth that can be found on food

rennet something that comes from an animal's stomach and is used to curdle milk

solid firm or hard with a shape

INDEX

Brie 19
factories 9
France 6
Germany 6
Gorgonzola 7, 16
mold 17
mozzarella 7, 18–19
Parmesan 14, 20–21
pasta 20
pizza 4, 20–21, 23